IT'S TIME

James Shafer

Acknowledgment

The purpose from me on these tw0 book reviews of Scripture is to show that a major foci of God's overview in the Bible is what has happened, what is happening, and then what will happen in the future. Since this information is communicated by life's Creator it is perfect in history, applicable in the present, and accurate in future happenings. The purpose of this prologue is to list sections of Scripture for you to read and appreciate that the Author has a plan and a roadmap.

THESE STAND OUT TO ME:

1)Matthew 24 2) Daniel 9 3) Zachariah 14 4) Ezekiel 38,39 6) 1 Thessalonians 4 and 2 Thessalonians 2 7) Isaiah 65:17+ and 66 7+ 8) Revelation 11 and 13 9) Revelation 20 and 10) Revelation 21 and 22!

This is a fascinating list of chapters and exciting to read. By reading these you will realize they are anything but exhaustive. They are mere snippets of the totality of renderings on the future of life and existence for all that God has created. They will demonstrate however, that God has, has had, and does have a plan: Jeremiah 29:10.

That's why I chose to briefly review the following books of Scripture. Daniel stands out as God disciplines Israel for breaking the ordained rules for resting the land. (Jeremiah 25: 11,12) God protects His people under judgment, and in particular saves His prophets from a fiery destruction as well as a den of lions. God then details the future prophesying the Empires that follow, the future Messiah, and the final judgment of mankind on earth.

In Revelation, God details the happenings of the determined 7 years, the death of billions, world leadership by the Godless, and our (the saved) lives in the most glorious location (Heaven) in created history. Please enjoy (?) this "brief" overview and better understand God's plan. And lastly, please understand my motivation given   the happenings of 2023, that living in this day and age we are certainly experiencing what leads me to the conclusion:

Dedication

Over the past 2 years my friend Tim Anderson (Pastor Tim) has rendered time to listen and correct some details in my "Briefs". I wish to acknowledge and thank him for his contribution. We have enjoyed the sharing of Southwestern experiences and family joys and … His input and time has been MUCH APPRECIATED!

About the Author

It all began in Rutherford New Jersey 80 years ago. After that, it was Battle Creek, Mi., Kansas, California, Denver, and Arizona. After 4 average college years, learning the most out of championship football, I spent another year of post graduate work looking at A's and B's. A struggled career ended up with a National Sales position, and the management, which I enjoyed.

Instead of accepting Law school in Chicago, I chose marriage, and spent the years studying the Bible. At long last I wished to share that, and thus my "1 Page Briefs" is here. My hope is to get readers introduced to God's Word without having to over read topics.

I think the sales career taught me to keep it simple, and get the order. My motivation was to share with my grandkids what I have learned over the years.

I am obviously not a scholar, but that is my advantage. My business success and failures have honed my skills and given me focus in life. I am just one man passing through. But maybe I will give someone a few good ideas for the trip; especially my grandkids!

Table of Contents

PROLOGUE 2023

The purpose from me of these two book reviews of Scripture is to show that a major focus of God's overview in the Bible is what has happened, what is happening, and then what will happen in the future. Since this information is communicated by life's Creator, it is perfect in history, applicable in the present, and accurate in future happenings. The purpose of this prologue is to list sections of Scripture for you to read and appreciate that the Author has a plan and a roadmap.

THESE STAND OUT TO ME:

1)Matthew 24 2) Daniel 9 3) Zachariah 14 4) Ezekiel 38,39 6) 1 Thessalonians 4 and 2 Thessalonians 2 7) Isaiah 65:17+ and 66 7+ 8) Revelation 11 and 13 9) Revelation 20 and 10) Revelation 21 and 22!

This is a fascinating list of chapters and exciting to read. By reading these, you will realize they are anything but exhaustive. They are mere snippets of the totality of renderings on the future of life and existence for all that God has created. They will demonstrate however, that God has, has had, and does have a plan: Jeremiah 29:10.

That's why I chose to briefly review the following books of Scripture. Daniel stands out as God disciplines Israel for breaking the ordained rules for resting the land. (Jeremiah 25: 11,12) God protects His people under judgment, and in particular, saves His prophets from a fiery destruction as well as a den of lions. God then details the future prophesying the Empires that follow, the future Messiah, and the final judgment of mankind on earth.

In Revelation, God details the happenings of the determined 7 years, the death of billions, world leadership by the Godless, and our (the saved) lives in the most glorious location (Heaven) in created history. Please enjoy this "brief" overview and better understand God's plan. And lastly, please understand my motivation given the happenings of 2023, that living in this day and age, we are certainly experiencing what leads me to the conclusion:

IT'S TIME! ☹ ☺

DANIEL #1
The Players 2022

I'm embarking on a "Brief" series referring to a book in the Old Testament named after its author. In my opinion, Daniel is one of 3 great men in scripture along with Job, and John the Baptist. There are a lot of great guys who were forgiven, transformed, and followed God with faithfulness and loyalty, but these 3 guys were almost born to be that way. I'm sure as kids, they were nerds. But as grown, dedicated, believers, they were special! Back to the Book of Daniel! The time frame is in the 500-600 BC's.

Israel was being carried off to Babylon for 70 years. Do you know why? They didn't rest their farmland every 7 years as instructed by God. It's detailed in 2 Chronicles 36:20, 21. Over 490 years, they chose, as an agricultural culture not to believe and obey the Creator. Is there anything that you've been ignoring over the past 50 years? Λ Please read Jeremiah 25!

The timeline is repeated in verse 11, including the King they will serve, and then God punishes the Chaldean Kings for doing what they did. Man, when God gets Mad…. Back to the Book of Daniel! There are 3 "gaves" in this 1st chapter: "God gave Jehoiakim king of Judah, into his (Nebuchadnezzar's) hand" (verse 2). "God gave Daniel favor and compassion in the sight of the chief of the eunuchs". This demonstrates God's activity in the daily activities of His creation, as well as the historical, and the entire creative process. As verses jump out at you in your study, grasp them close to your heart and brain, and Spirit. You also can cross that line of belief and faith, where you realize that every line of the Bible can be believed and applied to one's thinking, reasoning, and knowledge.

Back to the Book of Daniel! The 1st book then sets up the WHO of this prophetic writing. It revolves around Daniel and his 3 buddies.

His 3 buddies have 3 Jewish names and 3 Chaldean names. Look them up in chapter one. In verse 17, we read the 3rd "gave": "As for the 4 youths, God "gave" them learning and skill in all literature and wisdom, and Daniel had understanding in all visions and dreams". These 4 even told the chief eunuch what they would eat. No steak and eggs, they were vegetarians! HMMMMMMM! So the stage is set. The 70 years are rolling, just as prophesized. The players are in place. God's in the punishment program, and yet uses this period of time in captivity to predict the most profound human event in the history of mankind:

FASTEN YOUR SEATBELTS!

DANIEL #2
2022

The 1st half and lengthy diatribe of this chapter deals with King Nebuchadnezzar's dream. He has relied on advice from the King's inner circle, a group of men noted as magicians, conjurers, sorcerers, and Chaldeans. Sounds like Washington DC, to me. But He won't take their interpretations unless they can also reveal the dream first. If they don't, they're dead meat.

Daniel steps up. He reveals the dream and the interpretation, and it is a picture, in general, and in particular of coming world powers finalizing with Christ (the Rock). Nebuchadnezzar saw a giant statue in the dream and Daniel said it represented future kingdoms, including Babylon (the golden head), Persia, Greece, and what most agree to be Rome. They would all succumb eventually to the "ROCK". (verses 44, 45). Read 31-43 for the details of the statue and the kingdoms. In other words, the statue represented the world controlled by man's power, and the ROCK represented the world under the power of Jesus Christ. Get it?

And Daniel spoke a blessing in verses 20-23. In it, he noted that God picked and dethroned the Kings of all ages. The key in all of this, to me, is this giant statue revealed to King Nebuchadnezzar, was a picture, in detail, of the coming dynasties. They were powerful and valuable in the future, but nothing compared to the Rock of Jesus Christ, who would destroy them in the future and rule forever.

Nebuchadnezzar was so impressed that he made Daniel and his 3 buddies the rulers over the whole Babylonian province. But the King was fickle, as we see in the next chapter.

The other key share for me in this chapter is why Daniel is considered a prophet of God. In verses 19-23, God shares the dream with Daniel on a 75" flat screen TV (actually scripture calls it a night vision). He then praises God and extols Him for His majesty, greatness, and power. He ends in thankfulness. Ann Graham Lotz has written a nice commentary on "The Daniel Prayer" later on in chapter 9. We can now look backwards in history and see that Daniel was spot-on in prophetic history.

We can look at the Bible today and see God's outline for the future. Ezekiel speaks of the end of days when Israel will be scattered and then return. Is that the country of Israel I have seen in place since 1948? According to the Revelation, there's a 7-year period coming up that was spoken of in Daniel 9; looking ahead. WOW, this is a fascinating expose'. I can't wait to study the upcoming chapters. It's like a roller coaster ride; if you will.

FASTEN YOUR SEAT BELTS!

DANIEL #3 The Big Roast, or not!
2022

This chapter depicts the fiery furnace we've all heard about from the old Sunday school days. You know, that power, praise, and possessions can go to a man's head. King Nebuchadnezzar was no exception. This king had a statue erected that was made out of gold. Ninety feet high and 9 feet wide! This makes it 1/3 the size of the Statue of Liberty in New York, however, it was molded from gold. I can't imagine the value.

Now if that wasn't enough of an ego trip, the King demanded that when the music began playing at any time or anywhere, people were to face the statue and bow down and worship. That's exactly like today in the Middle East. Minarets blast loud music (noise) five times each day and Muslims are supposed to bow down to Mecca and worship Allah. Needless to say, Daniel and his buddies refused.

The loyalist leaders understandably obeyed the King and squealed at the Jewish non-compliers. The King wasn't just displeased, he was enraged. Shadrach, Meshach, and Abed-Nego told the King to pound sand, as they would only worship the God of creation and not Nebuchadnezzar or his phony gods. The King hated them and had them thrown into a furnace 7 times hotter than usual. The guards throwing them in were all burned to death. WOW! (that's hot)

The "Fickle" King then looked in and saw them walking around, with a 4th guy. King Nebuchadnezzar went near the furnace and called them to come out to safety. This wasn't 2020 folks, where we watch science-fiction on TV. This was a major departure from reality.

He proceeded to command the worship of this Jewish God (as he perceived Him), and no one would be allowed to be critical of their God. I guess He added God (the Creator) to his personal list.

This book by Daniel is great. The power of God is demonstrated in the daily lives of these brave believers. God gets real personal, as He did at the Red Sea, at Noah's Ark, at Jesus's Baptism, at the Crucifixion, at Paul's conversion, and finally at His return in the near future. There are many more times, but this one is really dramatic, especially in a totally Godless society (Kingdom).

At this point, Daniel's buddies were set for life! The king made sure they were prosperous from that time forward. He was indeed, impressed. Wouldn't you be? So all I can say in this day of Godlessness is to share your faith, share the Gospel, and stand firm in your testimony:

GO GET ROASTED!

DANIEL #4 NEBUCHADNEZZAR CHOPPED DOWN AND SAVED 2022

In this concluding chapter of King Nebuchadnezzar's reign, we see God's GRACE in action. The OT stories are depicted so that we see nothing new is going on today. This power hungry, vile, human King, who conquered the known world, murdered people, and took pride in his riches, was literally brought to his knees to eat grass and lose his mind. All the details are written in Chapter 4.

Daniel interpreted another of the King's dreams. He did it in humility as he said: "My Lord, if only the dream applied to those who hate you, and its interpretation to your adversaries" (vs 19). And then he spoke, "It is Heaven that rules" (vs 26). You need to read Chapter 4 and see Nebuchadnezzar's acceptance of this, and then he goes to his roof and takes total honor and praise for the Babylonian Empire.

Interpreters go in different directions in analyzing this chapter. One assumes Daniel took notes as Nebuchadnezzar spoke of his experience. This is no different than seeing Pharaoh quoted as he tangled with Moses. Another interpreter sees this chapter as being written by the King. I think that's a stretch, as the King was no prophet. Also it was noted that the magicians of the day "could not" interpret the dream. God gave the dream, and He could easily blind the eyes of all but Daniel. So I conclude that Daniel did interpret the dream "ALONE", and he did write down the King's thoughts and expressions.

It was, after all, dictated in form, substance, and detail, by the Holy Spirit;

But not a hill to die on!

GOD STRIKES HIM DOWN!

The dream plays itself out as the King eats grass and is cursed and helpless for 7 periods of time. Scripture pictures it as God chopping a tree down to a stump. Not sure by scripture if that's days, weeks, or "years". At any rate, when healed, the King blessed the God of creation in verse 34. He learned by verse 37 that: "He is able to humble those who walk in pride." The Holy Spirit said he would be protected with an iron or bronze fence until he was brought back to sanity.

Could you use a humbling? 25,000 people in this world die of starvation "EACH DAY", and I need to lose 30 pounds. Thousands live on the streets today, especially in warm climates, and I work on a new addition to my residence or a second house for the season. What does Nebuchadnezzar's life show us? Much like Solomon, we just don't handle prosperity and power that well as created beings.

Our culture has become so prideful, that we've forgotten our Genesis. We were created and born; out of the dust. We live and we die, through the GRACE of God. We need to share that GRACE as we prosper in life. There are plenty of neighbors out there that need our LOVE today. Don't be a Nebuchadnezzar and need to be admonished to reach goodness. "Choose for yourselves TODAY whom you will serve" (Joshua 24:15).

DON'T BE A TREE STUMP!

DANIEL #5
2022

I wanted to entitle this "Belshazzar the Pig", but it seemed inappropriate for a Bible commentary, even if true. King Belshazzar is the son/grandson of King Nebuchadnezzar in the first 4 chapters depending on the commentator. It was a couple three decades later and Nebuchadnezzar's recognition of the Creator God was long forgotten. This 30+ year old had multiple wives, and concubines, a besieged city, and decided to throw a party for 1000 sycophants.

They were crazy drunk and he decided to pull out the Jewish Temple artifacts of gold and silver to use for drinking. Be careful boys and girls, you might just make God mad. Been drunk in your life? I have. You get really stupid! Out of nowhere, some spooky hand appeared and began writing on the plaster wall. Please refer to Chapter 5 for the details. King Belshazzar wanted an interpretation, and the sorcerers were stumped again, all these years later.

The Queen's mother appeared, and suggested he call on Daniel, as his father had. (We assume mother, as all his "wives" were drunk by now) Daniel proceeded to interpret the word you can read in the 5th chapter of Daniel. Daniel said, "God has numbered the days of your Kingdom...you have been weighed...and found wanting...your Kingdom is divided" (Daniel 5: 26-28). Daniel castigated the smart aleck King for not remembering what his Dad/Grandpa went through and proceeded to say: Your time is up, you're a lightweight, and I'm splitting up Babylon to the next Kingdom. Belshazzar was dead that night.

Do we see parallels today? China, Russia, and India alone have Nuclear strength with hypersonic rockets our radar can't detect. We're getting drunk with alcohol and drugs, 30$ trillion in debt, and we murder a million unborn babies EACH YEAR! I find no problem with the King being wiped out. What about us??? Various writers speak of the Euphrates River that ran through the city being dammed up, so the Persians marched in on the dry river bed, opened the gates from within, and the party was over.

Constantly in Scripture, we see the ongoing battle between the Godless and the God fearing. The God fearing will always win, but you might not care for the process. I'll guarantee you that King Belshazzar didn't. Again, we see God actually participating in the details of human life. Many believers believe we are approaching one of those times again. He's always there, but sometimes it's most dramatic. 70 year old Daniel saw it again and will in the next chapter with the Lion's Den. Whatever the case, God's in the details:

DON'T BE A LIGHTWEIGHT!

DANIEL #6
THE LIONS DEN 2022

Any kid/person who has been through Judeo/Christian Sabbath School has heard 2 stories: David and Goliath and Daniel and the Lion's Den. This lion's den is an amazing picture of God's entering the cosmos, and affecting a believer's lifetime personally and hands-on.

You can read about Abraham, Jacob, Moses, David, Christ, and the disciples, but there is none more dramatic than God's encounter with Daniel in the Lions' den. In chapter 6, we again see the current ruler being aggrandized in his own mind by the ruling sycophant leaders of his day. They ask for a 30-day period of worship for the current King Darius, who signs an edict that he is obviously tricked into doing. The satraps (Congress) set up a form that no one would appeal to anyone but the ruler for petitions of grace, knowing full well their leader and "BOSS", Daniel prayed daily; petitioning the God of Creation.

He signed, Daniel prayed to God, and the punishment was to be thrown into a den full of hungry lions. Have you ever seen a set of Lion's teeth? They rip African buffalo to shreds with those teeth. Darius knew that Daniel had a spotless record and could be trusted with anything, including the money. When the crooked satraps exposed Daniel, the King was distraught. He knew he was tricked but he had to uphold the law of the Medes and Persians.

It says Daniel knew all about the edict and went to pray anyway. Have you read what has happened to church meetings during the pandemic of recent? And we're a democracy formed with Judeo-Christian principles and freedom. So Daniel was taken to the den that evening, and the King couldn't sleep! The King came in the morning, called out, and Daniel asked him to open the sealed den and extract him. The King was overjoyed and commenced to throw the satraps and their wives and children into the den. They were dead before hitting the bottom.

Lookout, Washington D.C.! I might add that just like his predecessors, Darius made up a poem/dictum to the God of Daniel; the "Living God". He stated: "His dominion shall be to the end, he who has saved Daniel." Again, God has persuaded a King, until the next Kingdom ☺ Those lions were hungry folks. I love the faith of old Daniel who was now over 70. He retired in luxury!

EAT YOUR HEARTS OUT; SIEGFRIED AND ROY

DANIEL #7 BACK TO THE FUTURE 2022

So we ended chapter 6 at the beginning of King Darius' reign around 520 BC. We then jump back to the 1st year of Belshazzar's term, around 30 years earlier. Daniel has another dream mentioned earlier, outlining the overall program for the future of civilization. For the born again believer, the Old Testament has prophecies throughout, noting details in the future that must/will take place. Chapter 7 screams them out.

The often quoted verses in Jeremiah 29: 11,12 spell out the Spirit of prophecy to Israel: "For I know the plans that I have for you, declares the Lord, plans for welfare and not for calamity, to give you a future and a hope. Then you will call on me, and come and pray to me, and I will listen to you!" The plan is summed up in verses 7: 13, 14. "One like a Son of man was coming…that all the peoples…might serve Him…and His Kingdom is one which will not be destroyed."

That, dear reader is like one being told you will someday be playing in the Super Bowl, and you will win the game. Jesus Christ will be the winning coach, but He will also be the referee. There will be 4 playoff games on the way to this finale' and all the "teams" will lose, no matter how successful they appear during the progress of the game. I will let you study the chapter to observe the play by play. Myriad books have been written as to the details of this chapter, from a now historical viewpoint as well as the prophetic.

So Daniel is now +/- 70 years old. He's been in Babylon for +/- 50 years. He witnessed the fiery furnace and his friend's salvation, He's been given the dream and interpretation of the same for Nebuchadnezzar, and he will experience his personal salvation from the Lion's Den in the future. All this time, I might add, Daniel is kept on top of the management heap. Every time he interprets the King's dream, he gets moved up over the local satraps or rulers, if you will.

15

The end is repeated in vs 25, where a world leader will speak out against heaven for 3 ½ years. That sounds like something I studied in the Book of Revelation. He's destroyed in vs 26, and the Highest one will take over in vs 27 and rule for an everlasting period.

Verse 28 ends the Revelation! "At this point, the revelation ended. As for me, Daniel, my thoughts were greatly alarming me and my face grew pale, but I kept the matter to myself". Daniel gets another vision 3 years later that is covered in Chapter 8. Suffice it to say, God's laying out the plan for the rest of life in advance. It goes to the end of times.

WITH THE EMPHASIS ON "END"

DANIEL #8
THE FUTURE FORETOLD 2022

This chapter really exemplifies the nature of this Bible, its author, and in particular, this Prophet and his writings. The author, God, Inspires the Prophet Daniel, (2 Timothy 3:16) and he writes what he is told concerning creation, the universe, and all that will happen in the next few years. One can't just read this like some fairy tale being made up, but see it as a direct communiqué' from our Creator, personally!

Chapter 8 moves forward to describe the next 3 iterations of world leaders in the Media/Persian, the Greeks, and then the 4 spin-offs. Lastly, a maniacal leader emerges who desecrates the Temple of Jerusalem and even mocks God by sacrificing a pig in the Holy of Holies. Life is not a cake walk as you well know. God has allowed ungodly leaders to rule from time to time, over history, as He lifts His hand of Grace and allows His adversary Satan to take over for a time, or times.

What gets to me is that the God of our created universe has just spelled out the future for the next 4- 500 years in the future. Once one appreciates the veracity of Biblical prophecy, the Bible becomes a miracle book of revelation. One can believe in the reality of creation, healing, science, salvation, birth, and everlasting life. I call it the process of transitioning from the known to the unknown. After decades of study, one comes to realize the reality of our Creator, and His miraculous and detailed involvement in our lives. Daniel receives, at his city approximately 200 miles east of Babylon, in Susa, where he is told through Gabriel the Angel, God's future blueprint for the world. WHY?

I accept that God is just laying down a framework already planned for the future like He said He would earlier. (Jeremiah 29: 11) For I know the plans I have for you...to give you a future and a hope? There are many prophesies in the Old Testament, many of which have been fulfilled; such as the Kingdoms and events listed in Daniel 8.

I am seeing many of the Ezekiel passages fulfilled today, as Israel has become a country for the Jewish people again in 1948. Do you think a visit from God is a casual thing? Daniel was sick for days. He also didn't get it. But we can! We've seen it happen already. We've seen other predictions take place also. A lot of what we refer to as prophecy, we now call history. What's our advantage then? We can search for the unfulfilled prophecies in Scripture and eagerly await them. It's a fun exercise, even if it makes you ill.

If we appreciate, however, that our God of creation is still active in the details of our existence, it's a beautiful thing. If we can pray to our God and know He is ever present, just as we can Google on our cell phones, it is sustaining, comforting, and keeps us expectant as we read about the Millennium, and Heaven at the end of Revelation in Scripture, and know what is "planned" for repentant born-again believers in the future.

THANK YOU, DANIEL! THANK YOU GOD!

DANIEL #9
JESUS IS PROPHESIED TO THE END
2022

For me, this is one of, if not the most significant, prophecies in the Old Testament. Another might be God telling Abraham about the Exodus 400 years in the future in Genesis 15. Another might be Micah 5 predicting the birthplace of the Messiah. Another is the 70 years of captivity noted in Jeremiah and Daniel. But in Daniel 9: 24-27, we see a dated prediction of 490 years of which all but seven are accounted for.

This isn't just amazing, it's absolutely incredible! So how did Daniel start this particular vision? He, of course, dated it and identified it as Darius's 1st year as King over the Babylonians (Chaldeans...522 B.C.). He quoted Jeremiah, who said the Jewish captivity was for 70 years (Jeremiah 29: 10). And then "I turned my face to the Lord God...I prayed to the Lord my God and made confession" (vs 3). I'm still looking forward to the day I can say that I prayed and fasted with any regularity. That would put me in the company of Daniel, Moses, David, and Jesus. That's quite a group.

Before the most significant prophecy in history, Daniel went on to confess his sins and pray for the sins of Israel. It's all in the 1st 19 verses of Chapter 9. Please read the above-mentioned and see if he wasn't praying for you and me also! The Angel Gabriel then appeared to Daniel, telling him how much Daniel was loved in Heaven, and imparted this detailed vision and time prophecy: "70 weeks (7X70 years = 490 years) are decreed for your people", "to put an end to sin" as judgment is completed and heaven is opened for Christ's saved. (that must speak of the end of this world, for sure). It predicts the death of Christ, and leaves 1 seven year period to be fulfilled.

I personally feel we are approaching that time period in 2022. I would that my grandkids could look forward to long lives filled with children, but that doesn't look probable as Israel has re-formed under Jewish rule, which is what the Bible refers to as the beginning of birth pains. Get the picture???

Vs 25 predicts from the time of King Artaxerxes until the Messiah's death is 483 years; as it was! Jerusalem will be rebuilt and in vs 26, Jesus will die, and the city will be destroyed by the Romans, and it was! In strange language, it states a desolation will occur with an individual signing a peace pack for the world until 3 ½ years are over and he enters the Temple as God until the true Creator God puts an end to it all and Christ returns (Zachariah 14, Matthew 24, 2 Thessalonians 2:8). This covers it all folks. It only takes +/-2500 years. It's capsulated in two verses, but true. Most of it has already happened.

CAN YOU SEE THE FINISH LINE?
PLEASE GET IN THE RACE

DANIEL #10
2022

These visions are coming decades apart, so the chapters of Daniel aren't chronological. What we see in chapter 10 is a Damascus road experience. Daniel gets a Word, fasts and prays for 3 weeks, and then sees a vision of a radiant angel. He alone sees the Angel, but those around him feel a trembling and run to hide. Daniel is on the bank of the Tigress River, so he does get around the kingdom. The last time we heard from him, he was at Susa. Another thing had changed over the years, Daniel was no longer a vegetarian, and he also drank wine.

Daniel felt led to pray, and had heard nothing after 3 weeks of prayer and fasting. The personality touched him and Daniel was weakened to falling down. The Angel explained that Daniel had been heard at the outset, but it took 21 days for the visitor to get through the battlegrounds fighting the prince of Persia. The Angel needed Michael to assist him in his passage. It's the same battle described in Ephesians 6:12. (We don't fight against flesh and blood)

The message conveyed to Daniel was that the Angel was off to fight the Prince of Persia so that the Prince of Greece could take over, just as Daniel had earlier foretold. This angelic visitation was quite debilitating to Daniel. The Angel again touched him to strengthen him. I'm not sure what the purpose was in this chapter/vision, but I do believe it was to communicate that a great deal is happening behind the scenes in a Spiritual dimension; constantly! It also conveyed that Daniel was "greatly loved" by Heaven.

The next chapter takes place 14 years later. Daniel was apparently a busy guy running the empire(s). Travelling from Babylon to Susa, and back, was no short venue in the day. Daniel was also around 70 years old, which was significant in those days. The Angel went off and joined Michael to introduce the Grecian Empire. I surmise that in the Spirit world, time was not a factor; but I speculate. The main thing to me is the connection between the two worlds (material and Spirit).

I sincerely believe God introduced the Book of Daniel to demonstrate God's power of intervention, and to lay out His plan for the next 2500 years. It seems to be rolling out according to plan.

DANIEL #11 2022

To me personally, Chapter 11 is the most difficult chapter in Daniel to digest. I've attached a couple of commentaries to help explain the details. It's basically an overview of the next +/- 500 years. It goes into extensive detail about powers from the North and South of Israel fighting each other. It touches on the desecration of the temple and the "abomination of desolation". It mentions attacks coming from the sea as well, and this "king" ruling the "beautiful Holy Mountain", and then coming to an end.

The attachments help un-confuse the picture, but what we see here is an overview of coming events. Why is that significant, you ask? Because it shows that God has plans down to the details of who's in charge, who will win, and who will lose in the future. At the time of Daniel's vision, it would have been total speculation and confusion. Today it has transpired, been noted historically, and gives us confidence in unfulfilled prophecy in our day. IT WILL HAPPEN!

As usual, Daniel starts with the date of the vision. It's been over a decade since his last encounter as Daniel continues in his task of ruling. I look forward to the other side, when I can review the life of Daniel, and see what kept him busy during these decades. He was a prominent ruler who never gave an inch on his faith, and lasted through 4 different rulers. That's beyond amazing. He must have been a brilliant manager. What I get out of this period of prophecy and history, is God's disgust with His chosen people and chosen land. Nations war back and forth over the top of Israel, and it ends up in the hands of Herod at the time of Christ. It's my understanding that the priesthood had left the lineage of Zadok, which was a Godly mandate.

This is why Christ so hated the Pharisees and Scribes of His day. The Book of Malachi castigates the leadership and unfaithfulness in Israel, and there is a 500 year period of deadness before the Gospels. So that's the story! That was the story, and that will be the story. I repeat that I feel personally that the purpose of this Book, and in particular, this chapter, is to point out that the artist of creation, our God and Savior, has created and designed, and planned the details of past and future history. I have, am, and will enjoy this trip to the fullest extent. Thank you, Daniel for being there! Thank you, God for using Daniel to share these messages! I believe the most fun part, good and bad, is yet to come;

ALLLLLLLLL ABOARD!

DANIEL # 12
THE END IS HERE 2022

And so, we come to a close for God's Prophet Daniel. He's around 100 years old, and I'm not sure if they retired in those years, but his tires were certainly worn bare. He's just heard the bad news from up North and back East. Today that could include Turkey, Russia, Iran, and China. UNSTOPPABLE! So God brings Michael back in, who God notes is the Spiritual Angel of the Jewish nation. It notes that this will be the "Time of the End", but Daniel is kept in the dark.

In the next section, we see a time period is laid out: 3 ½ years! Sound familiar? There are some times set up which do extend this particular holocaust, but it's basically the Great Tribulation. He further states that the wise will understand, and the wicked will act wickedly. I believe what one can see here is the emergence of Israel as a country with which to reckon. Without the Creator's involvement however, this is absurd. Ask Gideon, the warrior Prophet! We see this prophesied at the end of Amos 9: 11-15. "I will restore the fortunes of my people Israel" (vs 14), "and they shall never again be uprooted" (vs16)

Jesus covers the picture in Matthew 24, where He explains the details including the anti-Christ in the Temple (3rd), and the "Son of Man" coming on the clouds. In Ezekiel 47, we see the new topography, as Christ has returned for His 1000 year reign. Upon landing the 2nd Coming on the Mount of Olives, waters emerge and drain to the Mediterranean Ocean, and the Dead Sea. There is so much water spewing from the Temple base that the Dead Sea comes alive, and they catch fish in it.

As Paul and Barnabas came to the disciples in Acts 15, James confirmed to them, "I will rebuild the Tent (3rd Temple) of David that has fallen; I will rebuild the ruins."(vs 16). In Revelation 20, we see the return of Christ where all who refused the Mark of the Beast reigned with Christ for those 1000 years. What a glorious period of time for us believers. I think Isaiah covers the transition well in Chapter 66: 15-24. He brings judgment to unbelievers and Grace to believers. The focus will be "My Holy Mountain Jerusalem." (vs 20)

So God does speak with mystery, even to and through His prophets. He wants us to know, obviously, that a plan is in place. Not just a plan in general, but a plan with the specifics in place. I've jumped about to demonstrate this is more than happenstance. God brings up the future end times that have and will happen. Daniel's visions, prophecies, and experiences paint the picture of the past, present, and future. As it has taken place, we see God's involvement, even in lion's dens and fiery furnaces. Nothing more is necessary to prove the veracity of future predictions.

So God tells Daniel that the final time period will be 3 ½ years. He tells Daniel sacrifices will take place until the Abomination of Desolation takes a seat in the new Temple. He tells Daniel that a few more days will be added, however no one seems to know what is involved in that extra few days. God keeps mysteries. Christ even said: "only the Father knows the day and the hour" (Mark 13:32). And God closes His revelation to Daniel: "And you shall rest and you shall stand in your allotted place at:

THE END OF DAYS'!
IT'S COMING, DEAR READER!

REVELATION REVEALED #1
2023

The world doesn't really need another commentary on the Book of Revelation. But I feel it would be well served with a few "Briefs". This shortened version will be set up to isolate and identify key concepts by chapter in a brief and understandable version: "REVELATION IS RELEVANT IN 2023" The time of buying and selling needing numbers (credit cards) has arrived (bitcoin). There is the experience of worldwide communication as we have today instantly in Revelation (as with satellites).

There is aggressive planning to construct a physical Temple again in the land of Israel, a country which exists as an entity again. The Temple was destroyed when Revelation was written. There is worldwide hatred and the desire for warring nations to wipe out the Jewish state, which ceased to exist at the time of this writing of the Apocalypse. I have read over a dozen books on the subject, and most were thick. The most famous one in my years was the Lindsey commentary: "The Late Great Planet Earth". We will filter this great book of prophecy as briefly as possible for the purpose of communicating salient points from this normally very confusing book.

I'll let the intellectuals delve into the enormous detail of future events. I just want to communicate an understandable overview. Please understand that God has plans for our world's judgment (punishment). Society breaks the 10 Commandments with impunity. Eventually, GOD will act. He gave us indicators of the times that are/were coming, and it looks like we're getting close. (MATTHEW 24) If you read the story about Noah, he spent 120 years building the Titanic Ark, until finally taking his family of 8 on board, and God closed the door. 8 people were saved, and millions perished in death and judgment from the flood.

Hopefully these following "Briefs" on God's revelation of the future will help in your understanding of these most significant warnings and blessings from our Creator for the NEAR future.

DON'T WAIT FOR THE DOOR TO SHUT!

REVELATION REVEALED #2
Chapter 1 2023

John is picked by Christ for this Revelation of the Apocalypse. He is the last Apostle to live and has been banished to an Island called Patmos. Evangelist Greg Laurie visited this God forsaken pile of rocks and filmed the location, and it's hard to believe one could last for any period of time. Assuredly at this point in John's 90+ years, he should be in the assisted living home now and not climbing rocks and living in a cave. And yet Christ came to him and instructed him to "write in a book." (vs 1:11)

As best as John could describe, this vision and appearance of Christ was as "burnished bronze that glowed as in a furnace, and His voice was as the sound of many waters". That makes me think of waves pounding the many shores that I visited, from Hawaii to California, to the Atlantic on our East Coast, or Portugal, to name a few of my experiences. Needless to say, Christ's apparition was an amazing experience for John as Christ said in verses 17 and 18, "I am the 1st and the last, and the living one; and I was dead, and behold, I am alive for evermore". Do you really appreciate what Christ communicated here?

If you learned nothing more from reading Scripture, hang on to this revelation: Christ lived, Christ died, Christ rose from the dead, and Christ demonstrated that life is eternal. To this believer, the whole point of Revelation is to demonstrate that God not only communicated past history perfectly, but has now begun the process of perfect history "IN THE FUTURE". As we read Chapter #1, we see God revealing the future to John, on the Island of Patmos, to a trusted, rubber meets-the-road educated disciple; for our benefit. One unanswered question for me, on the other side, is what John's writing materials were?

I know he didn't have a word processor or copy machine. What, no spell check? Christ also detailed messages to the seven noted churches, their seven "guardian" ANGELS, and the future for the OVERCOMERS. One exhortation of which to take note is in verse 3: "Blessed is he who reads and those that hear this prophecy, and heeds the things which are written in it; for the time is near. I believe that is more relevant than ever in 2023. As I overview this amazing promised apocalypse, I believe the reader and newly acquainted Bible student with being blessed with God's promises in this age!

DON'T JUST GO TO CHURCH, BE AN OVERCOMER
1 John 5:1-5

REVELATION REVEALED #3
CHAPTERS 2, 3 2023

In chapter one, Christ listed the churches He wanted letters written to in verse 11. In chapters 2, 3 He went into the content that He wished to communicate. These were fellowships in existence at the time of writing, which each had good and bad practices.

In each instance, Christ identified His attributes of glory and explained that there were always people who were saved (overcomers) no matter how badly the parishioners acted or believed. Christ shared His Devine attributes to witness to each church (ecclesia): Ephesus: The one who holds the 7 stars in His right hand, the One who walks among the 7 golden lamp stands… Smyrna: The 1st and the last, who was dead, and has come to life… Pergamum: the one who has the sharp two edged sword… Thyatira: The Son of God, who has eyes like a flame of fire, and His feet are like burnished bronze… Sardis: He who has the seven Spirits of God, and the seven stars… Philadelphia: He who is Holy, who is true, who has the key of David, who opens and no one will shut, who shuts and no one will open… Laodicea: The Amen, the faithful and true witness, the Beginning of the creation of God…

The criticisms listed were applied based on illicit sins and practices in each fellowship. Some scholars see this as contemporary to John's life and some see these as different ages looking forward over the next 2000 years. No matter what, we see church development, belief, and practice for future years. It's sad to see the way sin works its way into the Christian community. But make no mistake, salvation is the result of Christ's sacrifice, and will never be erased from the believer's heart; FOR ETERNITY (It's called the "NEW" covenant).

But sin will continue in this life, and we must battle this internal inclination until the end. Christ followed up by calling out the saved, born-again of each flock. God called out these fellowships (ecclesia) but recognized that all involved would not be saved. Those that were, were given promises for eternity. As you read about each church, take note of the promise given for OVERCOMING/CONQUERING!

BE AN OVERCOMER!
1st JOHN 4-6

REVELATION REVEALED #4
CHAPTERS 4, 5
2023

John now took a trip to Heaven. In the Spirit or in the flesh, he was given a vision of the greatness of Heaven and the glory of Christ. Remember Paul's trip? (2 Corinthians 12:2) "After these things I looked, and behold, a door standing open in Heaven…and the 1st voice I had heard like the sound of a trumpet speaking with me said, "Come up here"… (Chapter 4:1) He then saw Christ "sitting on the throne." (vs 2)

At this stage, we read about all sorts of symbols and animals and people praising their Creator singing, "Holy, Holy, Holy is the Lord God Almighty, who was, and who is, and who is to come." John was as encouraged as am I: "Stop weeping, behold the Lion who is from the tribe of Judah, the root of David, has overcome so as to open the Book and its seven seals." (vs 5)

So what are these seals all about? The Tribulation is about to begin and the judgments on earth will follow. The seven seals are the beginning, and Christ is the arbiter. In verses 6 and 7, John sees a Lamb standing who retrieves the Book of the seven seals from the One sitting on the throne. We now see a cacophony of worshippers adoring the Lamb, playing the harps, and smelling the incense (prayers) of God's Saints. It is a beautiful time of praise and worship as Christ begins the process of judgment over mankind.

In vs 11, we see John's vision of the myriads in worship. We're talking about millions or billions dear reader. We are speaking of created beings going back to the time of Adam and Eve. Just check out the genealogies listed in Scripture. (Luke 3) The thrill of being there without a sinful nature and with full mental capabilities will be the epitome of my created existence. I can't wait to hear my heavenly voice. ☺

The whole point of chapters 4 and 5 is to picture the glory and power of the risen Christ in heaven. He will reign forever and ever. He has earned, if you will, the "power of judgment" and the ability of opening the seals to begin the process. ONLY HIM!

If you happen to accept the timing of the "Rapture" from 1 Thessalonians 4:16, 17, you will see this vision as our trip to heaven and the experience of God's glory and worship in heaven. As it was for John and Paul, and all the dead in Christ, it is magnificent. There will be total mental acumen, no sinful nature, no depression, and perfect health. No crying, no animosity, and NO DEATH! I will sing like Andrea Bocelli, run like Usain Bolt, and play golf better than Tiger Woods ever could.

Heaven is wonderful, glorious, and everlasting for those of us who accepted Christ's sacrifice. Have you? We will finalize this quick commentary in chapters 21 and 22. The point here is that heaven is a beautiful place, experience, location, and the ticket for entrance is repentance, NOW! Don't miss the glory described in these 2 chapters. Go to the party, and the next 13 chapters will describe what people live and die through who miss the RAPTURE mentioned above.

CONFIRM YOUR RESERVATION!

REVELATION REVEALED #5
CHAPTER 6 2023

Let the TRIBULATION begin. Chapters 6-19 focus on the period prophesied in Daniel 9:27. God notified us through the Prophet Daniel that a great Tribulation would take place at the end of the age before the Millennium. He said there would be a 7 year period when God would judge the earth for its sins. Paul let us know in the New Testament that it wasn't set up for believers, as they would trust in Christ for their judgment and forgiveness.

Christians will be "snatched away" from this judgment, having trusted in Christ, and chapters 6-19 would then unfold. There are 3 sets of occurrences to unfold called the Seal judgments, the Trumpet judgments, and the bowl judgments. They are nasty, earthshaking, and deadly. At the end, over half of the earth's population will be killed, the economy will bottom out, and eating and drinking will end for a time. Thank God that the time period will only be 7 years.

Chapter 6 begins with the "SEAL" judgments. They are: 1) The antichrist suits up on a white horse. He has a bow and no arrows as I believe he will emerge as a peacekeeper after the disruption caused by Rapture. Going back to Daniel, he has the world power to set up a peace pact. 2) The rider on the red horse comes forth and wars break out. 3) The rider on the black horse is let out and famine follows him worldwide. 4) 25% of the population dies. Between the rapture and this figure, we are looking at 3 BB less people. 5) I love this one. People can still be saved in the tribulation. A new movie was just released called "Left Behind", which deals with those who have been saved and martyred during this period. Halleluiah! 6) Cosmic convulsions take place from earthquakes on this planet to replacements in the celestials.

The above would be more than enough for me or any human being alive at the time. But this is only the beginning. Keep in mind; this will only be an overview for anyone interested that can't absorb a text or 2 inch thick documentary. I wish to share a description of the Apocalypse, and not an in depth study of the details. I want to communicate that God loves His creation but can't abide SIN without retribution at some point.

IT HAS BEGUN!

REVELATION REVEALED #6
CHAPTER 7
2023

In this chapter, we see the unleashing of evangelism as never before. 144,000 men of the Jewish race were saved and sent. They are located throughout the world, I'm sure. They are attached to 12 different tribes that, for some reason, don't align with Jacob's sons (Genesis 30) or the tribes listed in Ezekiel 48. God lists them; I accept! Some well meaning Christians think that God is done with the Jews as their rejection of the Messiah was replaced by Christian believers. I believe God's noting of Revelation 7 proves the extension of the Abraham Covenant.

I was led back to Hosea in the Old Testament for perspective. The picture of God and Israel was illustrated by the marriage of Hosea, the Prophet to Gomer, the whore. It's covered in the 1st 3 chapters. Hosea is a hard read and the illustration is hard to comprehend. God is picturing how Israel whores itself out to Baal and the gods of their day and He is livid. Imagine; Baal worships involved baby sacrifice and climate control. Sound familiar?

In this exposition through Hosea, God states His positions to the Israelites: "There is no Savior besides me" (13:4). "I will ransom them from the power of Sheol" (13:14). "Take words with you and return to the Lord. Say to Him, Take away all iniquity" (14: 2). We know our God forgives, and it's not just for us under the New Covenant already. In chapter 7, we see the 144,000 saved and all those who accepted their testimony. Yes, people do get saved in the Tribulation 7 year period. (vs 14)

At the beginning of the chapter, God has the angels cut off the wind. I don't think we appreciate how involved God is in the day to day of our lives. Global warming isn't based on man's activities, but

God's! In verse 16, He notes that "neither shall the sun beat down on them nor any heat". Christ then moves to the center of the throne and "guides them to springs of the waters of life; and God shall wipe every tear from their eyes."

By now, we have seen 1-2 BB Christians removed and roughly 2 BB non-Christians killed. That number could reach up to ½ of today's population. At the same time, we have 144,000 Jewish Billy Grahams running around, which explains the new Tribulation saints mentioned in 7: 13 and 14. It's a terrible time, and it's a beautiful time. People are suffering from the opened Seals, and people are being saved and martyred to Heaven.

God does forgive, and I believe this re-establishment with the Jewish race exemplifies that activity. The Abrahamic Covenant was one-sided which Abraham happened to have slept through. The Nordic Covenant was also established by God, and guarantees against worldly destruction by flood no matter what the Global Warming people of our day have to say.

So let your resistant, rebellious acquaintances and relatives know: when you disappear as Christ did in Acts 1, tell them to get on their knees. God will still forgive them, just as He will the new evangelists. Listen early on as the 2 witnesses in chapter 11 proclaim the Gospel. But whatever you do:

LISTEN!

REVELATION REVEALED #7
CHAPTERS 8,9,10 2023
DOOM AND GLOOM

The world now experiences the 7 trumpets. This will be a period of misery, destruction and death. The trumpets are: 1 1/3 of all vegetation destroyed, 2 1/3 of the sea turned to blood, fish die, and ships destroyed, 3 the fresh waters on earth will be destroyed, 4 the sun, moon and stars darkened, 5 people will be tormented by locust for 5 months released from the abyss. And 6, an army of 200,000,000 will be released from the East and 1/3 of mankind will die.

You can just read the chapters, but do understand, this is no time to be on planet Earth. I appreciate God's love, forgiveness, and care, but I don't want His judgment and punishment. These 3 chapters are enough to drive anyone to repentance and yet: "they did not repent of their murders nor of their sorceries nor of their immorality nor of their thefts" (9: 21). Thank God that those of us who have trusted in Christ, believed in the Gospel, and repented of our sins, will already have left the surface of the earth just like Christ did in Acts: 1. Take your time, read through these chapters. When God has had enough, He's had enough.

Have you ever had a stupid rebellious child? You put up with them and put up with them, and it's finally time for the belt or the woodshed. I've been there, and I've also been that child. Please repent if you are reading this. It's no accident you're reading this, you know? Receive God's Grace, and miss the tumult of these 3 chapters. It's scary and indeed ugly! Please note that in these trumpet judgments, roughly 2 BB people die off of the earth's crust. Life on earth will end for all, but life will continue in the new existence. (Daniel 12: 2, Luke 16).

It's a new world my friend with Christians removed, a Godless world leader in charge, AI fully activated, and devastating natural disasters activated. You don't want to be here. We will move forward now for the final set of God's judgments called the Bowl Judgments. The 2 witnesses evangelize, the currency is digitized, Satan is finally kicked out of heaven, and people's permanent marks are issued. You've been warned! It's not too late! It's time to repent:

GET SAVED!

REVELATION REVEALED #8
CHAPTER 11
2023

When God speaks of the future, it is literal to Him. As we read it, sometimes it's confusing and figurative. Revelation 11 is a great example of that. The most significant and realistic part is that of the two witnesses. These 2 representatives for God are seen throughout the world and testify of God and Jesus Christ. The people of the world hate them and especially their message.

At John's time, one might wonder at anyone outside of Jerusalem knowing about them. In our age, it is easy to see them on CNN or any world streaming network. I thought of the day I viewed the airplanes hit the twin towers. I was in Seattle. How about the day that Notre Dame in Paris went up in flames? I watched it from my TV chair as I remembered visiting that church multiple times. We live in the same time, and see it now capability today.

I'm timing these two evangelists at the beginning of the Great Tribulation. They are referred to as olive trees and lampstands. Zachariah 4 refers to olive trees and in verse 14 as "anointed ones, who are standing by the Lord of the whole earth." The lampstands I read as those called out, to fellowship: ecclesia. They prophesy for 3 ½ years or exactly ½ of the 7 year tribulation period. We know that people get saved in the 7 years since Rev 7: 14 says so. This further shows that the Book of Revelation isn't sequential or linear.

So they evangelize the world, and the people who take on Satan's mark hate them. God releases Satan from the abyss, and he is allowed to kill them. It happens in Jerusalem and they are left there for 3 ½ days. That's pretty ugly dear reader and shows how deprived and ungodly people become. Keep in mind as we read in chapter 9, that 1/3 of civilization has already died. So at this point, 1BB + have been

41

raptured, 2BB + have now perished from calamities and pestilence, and people are still happy the witnesses are killed. Go get em, Senator Bernie Sanders.

The chapter ends with the awakening and rapture of the 2 witnesses. Yes my friend, life is forever. To punctuate, God blows the 7th trumpet, and the glories are envisioned and the judgments are brought on. As God opens the heavens in all their glory and the wonderful ARK of salvation, He continues to castigate the unregenerate.

Whatever you do, place your faith in Christ. God does run out of patience and mercy for the unbelievers. He does execute judgment, as we are seeing here. But as a loving and merciful creator, He keeps extending His Grace. In the midst of this great 7 year period, people still repent and ask forgiveness. In a short time, we will have the opportunity to enjoy eternity. I look forward to seeing you there.

REVELATION REVEALED # 9
CHAPTER 12 SATANS DOWNFALL
2023

There comes a point at which God no longer tolerates Satan's presence and criticisms of the earthly saints in Heaven. That's correct, just as Satan was shown in Job 1 to be one of those allowed in God's domain, and one who could "roam about on the earth", God now expels Satan from Heaven and as the saying goes, the jig is up.

The captain of rebellion and stupidity is now earthbound and proceeds to attack God's chosen land and seed! This once champion of the Heavenly musical realm (be careful what you sing), was captioned in Isaiah 14 and Ezekiel 28. It was noted in Matthew 4 that God used him to tempt Christ 3 times after Christ spent 40 days without food in the wilderness. It's AMAZING, that Christ could resist, and that Satan could be that stupid to actually go after God the son. But the time has arrived and the last 7 year period is ½ way through and God is pulling out all the stops. Bible scholars (especially dispensationalists) see this as the beginning of the last 3 ½ years as God divides the TRIBULATION up.

Satan loses a significant battle with the Archangel Michael in the heavens, and is thrown down to earth taking 1/3 of all the angels with him. No! I don't get it either, but John describes it in chapter 12, and I believe it. Surprisingly, the statement is made in verse 12 that Satan is really upset (church words) because he knows he only has a short time. That amazes me, but I know what the next few chapters describe. So we now see Satan on the attack. He goes after Israel which re-establishes in the 1900's, but God whisks the believers to safety on the wings of eagles as pictured in Exodus 19:4, and Deuteronomy 32:11.

Remember the parting of the Red Sea and the manna in the wilderness. All I can say without enormous detail is that Satan's bound to earth, he goes after the reset Israel, and any Jewish person on earth at this future time. (vs 17) Satan will be finished and locked up in 3 ½ years after the worst set of destruction known to mankind since Noah's flood. He will be jailed in the abyss until the end of the Millennium, and released to raise havoc one last time before his time of judgment, ETERNAL fire and being eaten by WORMS, in the domain of hell! (Revelation 20:10)

GOODBYE SATAN! FOREVER!

REVELATION REVEALED # 10
CHAPTER 13
ANTICHRIST, THE WORLD LEADER

"It was the best of times, it was the worst of times"—Dickens. Back in "my day", A Tale of Two Cities was a must read in history class. We had certain classics to read that rounded out our sense of history (that repeats itself), and just plain good writing and expression. We face that prophesized period of history in the making today. Cataclysmic events are noted in Daniel 9, Matthew 24, 1 Thessalonians 4, and Revelation 4, which we covered earlier.

God has a history for judgment in Scripture when He has reached the end of His mercy with non-believing humans and it seems to be approaching us again. When Noah sailed, God rescued 8 people. When God blasted Sodom and Gomorrah, only Lot and his family escaped. When God finally judges our civilization, and He will, Bible believing saints who have trusted God through Jesus Christ will be extracted (removed) before He renders the World's deserved punishment. (It's called the Rapture) Just as warmth is assured by the Sun, just as light is assured by the moon at night, and death is assured by life, so judgment will be exercised in our sinful society. ARE YOU PREPARED?

In chapter 13, we see the reorganization of society. The world moves to a singularly purposed government run by a maniacal individual God calls the antiChrist; for a good reason. In 2023, we can see all the trappings of interdependence and a singular world society and politic! If all Christians are removed like Lot and Noah, the scene is wide open for leadership to take over with all those pesky and irritating Christians gone. IT WILL HAPPEN! And soon, I believe. Are we in the "Roaring 20's again? Is the "Crash" fast approaching? Are World leaders juxtaposing for a takeover? I think the news stories would support the premise.

45

So chapter 13 gives us two major happenings: A world leader, who comes into prominence, is attacked and killed, and rises from the dead to lead the population to destruction. He is supported in the effort by his crony, the False Prophet, as a caddie supports a professional golfer. The means for financial control is a digital system for buying and selling. As I write this scenario, a large bank on the West Coast has just failed, causing $BB's in losses. It's not that bad things happen or will happen; it's how world leaders will correct the problem without God's input in the future. Remember the World Trade Center? By means of energy management, climate control, population explosion and control; how do non-believers in our Creator approach problems today?

Back in the seal judgments (Chapters 6&7), we see that people will still be saved in the Great Tribulation. Praise the Lord. But set your mind on the fact that God has predicted the future as accurately as He has detailed the past. Christians will be snatched off the earth's surface, a powerful despot will take over world leadership (the antichrist) and your finances will be changed to digital control with the extension of life control. Read Chapter 13 over again. Read it until you get (comprehend) it. He's coming folks and the world's Ark is all ready:

TO FLOAT. ☹

REVELATION REVEALED # 11
CHAPTERS 14, 15
2023

All hell breaks loose. People are dying and God is judging. For 3 ½ years under a one world government, this ruler has developed power and control, world acclaim, and reverence. Part of the program is the demand for subservience and worship. Manipulation is founded and endorsed in chap 13:16-18. You must read Daniel 9: 27, 2 Thessalonians 2: 3, 4, and Matthew 24: 15 and get the picture. This world leader will gain adoration and worship as he dies and lives again (chap 13: 3, 4) so that he actually claims to be god.

From here then, it's a downhill slide! Have you ever skied? It's a beautiful sport, and depending on the slope, it's a slow run or measurably FAST. Without moguls, one can speed out of control. Chapters 14 and 15 image the 144,000 again as the world evangelists having been blessed with their heavenly trips. Some interpret them to be the Jewish believers from chap 7, and others, a new group. I believe the exact same number speaks volumes, and also I believe it fulfills Jeremiah 31: 31-34. There are lots of opinions in these reflections of prophecy.

Chapter 14:6 shows that the whole world will hear the Gospel; "To every nation and tribe and tongue and people". That covers it! The earth is warned as angels fly around with the messages: "Fear God and give Him glory, because the hour of judgment has come" (chap 14), "Fallen fallen, is Babylon"(world system), "Don't take the MARK, or go to hell". It then pictures Christ on a cloud swinging a sickle. Don't chuckle as He swings that sickle and the blood flows; lots of blood dear reader. (vs 20) That covers 200 miles or the distance from Jerusalem to Damascus. It also says to the horse's bridles. This preview of Armageddon is scary and not limited to the plain of Megiddo that I visited once. Praise God for chapter 15 as "the wrath of God is finished" (chap 15: 1) Salvation is witnessed and He compares the BB's of saved people in Heaven to a sea of glass. It's a beautiful image!

It's incredible that the saved in heaven begin singing the "Song of Moses". If you turn to Exodus 15 you will read this beautiful passage sung as the Israelites escaped the army of Egyptian soldiers after passing through the Red Sea. It's an amazing commentary on human memory and appreciation that the Jewish people could see a miracle that grand, having walked on the dry ground across the Red Sea only to see the waters collapse on the army chasing them. Their response: forget about it in a couple of days. Read Exodus 15.

Now they sing that song in Heaven, and remember. ☺ Has the Red Sea ever parted for you in this life? Did you remember the times? Bank 'em and draw on your account in the future. My go-to verses are Matthew 6: 25-34. Back in the early 70's, I lost it all ($$), I learned these verses and swore I would never get uptight about finances again. I still haven't!

We are now introduced again to the Heavenly Tabernacle. God's still got some work to do on earth, and it isn't pretty; the bowls of judgment. No one can enter the Heavenly Temple until it's over. But we at least get a glimpse of Heaven and our eternal future.

BE THERE ☺

REVELATION REVEALED # 12
CHAPTER 16 2023
ALL HELL BREAKS OUT

In this chapter, God yells out from His Heavenly Temple to pour out the 7 bowls of wrath. Remember that the 7 seals have been opened by the Lamb (Jesus), and the 7 trumpets have been blown already. Now He unleashes the 7 Bowls of judgment as listed: 1) Sores, 2) seas turn to blood, 3) all fresh waters turn bloody, 4) terrible heat from the sun, 5) supernatural darkness, 6) Euphrates river dries up, and 7) major earthquakes and 100# hailstones.

This shows that Revelation isn't linear or sequential. The Battle of Armageddon is mentioned here requiring an army from the East of 200,000,000 written about in chapter 9. They needed the "dry Euphrates" to march to the Middle East. In chapter 14:20, we already read about Armageddon's results: 200 miles of blood up to the horses bridles. This is an ugly picture, dear reader but the results of 1000s of years of sin, and God's mercy to the earth. It was now time for God to act, AGAIN!

So in this chapter God now all but destroys the world we know and live on. John speaks of Islands moving and mountains not being found. He speaks of unbelievably huge hailstones, and electrical storms. To live at this time will be beyond the pale. I might remind you that almost half the population of the earth will die. The amazing thing is that as a result people will still blaspheme God, their Creator. God finally cuts things off as it would eventually eliminate mankind. (Matthew 24: 22) This chapter closes with two savage attacks that no man could or will be able to defend; earthquakes beyond experience, mountains leveling, and 100# hailstones.

Remember that we live on this very large ball (8000 miles in diameter), but only reside on the crust. Shaking this earthly ball might just dislodge the Pacific Rim. Goodbye California, Japan, and Australia! AND NEW YORK CITY? The results will be catastrophic! Enough already!

Those on the earth are the ones LEFT BEHIND! These are the non-believers and blasphemers! I feel badly for them all, but chapter 20 is coming! It only leads me to appreciation and devotion that I've been blessed with the Grace of Salvation and have already been taken away in chapter 4. Hear these words and admonitions, and be saved from all of the above.

REVELATION REVEALED #13
CHAPTERS 17, 18 2023
BABYLON FALLS

The next 2 chapters speak of a time when the world system crumbles. The main feature is the destruction of distribution. In a world dependent on the flow and interchange of products and provisions, a stoppage to that is cataclysmic. In the last 20 years of my career, I focused on the distribution of cash registers in my company. They were made at the factory with "just-in-time" parts and pieces. That means pieces of inventory like shells, computer boards, and keytops had to arrive as the register proceeded down the production line.

A box had to then be at the line's end to house the completed unit. It was shipped off and the moment it was offloaded from the sea-faring vessel, we could count our recorded sales. This is how cars are made, beef is processed and clothes are distributed. Ask your grandchildren where corn comes from and they will probably say the Safeway store. People today are in love with and dependent on the world's system of distribution. They organize kingdoms, and obey the leadership, whether good or evil. But in God's judgment, these Godless leaders will fail in spades, allow chaos, and gradually but dramatically take down the world economic system.

All I need do is describe the decline of our country's morality in 2023, and we can see Revelation 17. You can now read it for yourselves. There are 2 key verses for me. Verse 8 describes the leadership of Satan, who "was and is not, and is about to come up out of the abyss and to go to destruction". Verse 14 says, "These will wage war against the Lamb". This is the great conflict/war between Christ and Satan worked out in the world scene. In chapter 18: 9-14, we see the whole program fall apart. Don't be surprised, God's judging our Godless system. In verses 16 &17, we see described the loss of wealth.

Those of you stashing cash in gold and silver will be very disappointed. It will be worthless. This awful legacy will be consummate in verse 24, when blame will be laid for the death of the prophets and saints over history. As a matter of fact, in verse 20, the "saints, apostles, and prophets" will rejoice. I have read a dozen commentaries, listened to a dozen teachers, and participated in many Bible studies, and I can assure if these chapters confuse you, you're in good company.

Why? God wants it that way and I'm sure it was even more confusing when John wrote it. Believe it however, that judgment is coming. Roughly 4 BB people will be dead or gone in the 7 years of TRIBULATION. The crust of the earth has been reshaped, Christ is about to return, and the current inhabitants of the earth will be devastated and ready for a Savior. We will soon see that one is coming.

Read these chapters with the above overview in mind. Everything we take for granted will become as a 3rd world country. People will die, rivers will turn to blood, the distribution system will crumble, and leadership will disintegrate. One exciting afterthought however, if you have reconciled with God, through Christ is that you get to miss all this. Read these 2 chapters again; repent; look to your Creator and for sure:

GET SAVED! ☺

REVELATION REVEALED #14
CHAPTER 19
2023

HALLELUIAH

Halleluiah seems to be an odd exclamation at this point. But it's coming out of Heaven, and it's stated/sung at the end of God's destruction of the economy and man's distribution system. But that's what we will be singing! And why? "Because His judgments are true and righteous."(vs 2) In verse 4, John is shown the 24 Elders and 4 living creatures. As to their definition, there isn't a consensus. My take on it is they made the Hall of Fame. Maybe some were Prophets, maybe disciples, or maybe martyrs?

I played football for 7 years in high school and college. I lettered 6 of the 7; I was 1st string 3 of the 7; I didn't make all American or the Hall of Fame. Looking back, I was thrilled to be on those teams (and soon the Heavenly team). I was more thrilled to start and get letters of recognition for participation. I can't wait to arrive someday because I am just part of the team!

Verses 7-10 speak of the marriage in Heaven. Who's getting married? Christ marries all of His believers. You can read about it in Ephesians 5: 22-33. You consent to the relationship when you repent of your sins and get baptized. You leave earthly relationships and join Jesus Christ in the heavenlies. And now you see the reason(s) for singing the halleluiah again and again and again!

We then move toward the finale! Christ mounts a white horse and we join with Him. To me, this is all figurative, but we are returning LITERALLY! On Christ's thigh is written: "KING OF KINGS and LORD OF LORDS" (vs 16). We return again to Chapter 14:20, where we see Armageddon with blood up to the horse's bridles for 200 miles. No wonder an angel called up scores of birds to eat the dead flesh.

Verse 19 points out the earthly rulers drawn to fight against Christ and our army.

Verse 20 and 21 are ugly, but convicting. The two world leaders are seized and thrown into the lake of fire, ALIVE, and Christ eliminates the rest of their followers, then flies the birds to clean up the mess. Jesus Christ is now the championship leader that the disciples were hoping for in Acts 1:6.

So Halleluiah, my fellow believers! In the beginning, God creates the universe and its people. In the end, He returns for the Super Bowl of existence and takes home the trophy. THAT'S EXCITING! But hold on for a Millennium. We have 1000 years to go. Jesus will stick around and manage things out of Jerusalem. (Zachariah 14) We'll cover the details in the next "Brief". In the meantime:

SADDLE UP COWBOYS AND GIRLS! ☺

REVELATION REVEALED #15
CHAPTER 20
2023

IT'S TIME

Yes it's time, dear reader. I'm amazed at the way God set up the Scripture with the actual beginning in Genesis 1-3 and the ending in Revelation 19-22. He began with Moses writing about Adam through God's dictation, and ended through John being dictated to by the Holy Spirit. We just finished with the infamous battle of Armageddon, and Jesus Christ's return to earth: WITH US! (True believers) Christ locks up Satan in the abyss (prison) and the 1000 years begins. 1000 years is stated 5 times.

I learned years ago in one of my management positions, the need for planning. It's actually a God thing. He shows us His planning perfection which we call prophecies. There are 100's, but I'll list three. In Genesis 15:13 He tells Abraham that his chosen descendants will be enslaved for 400 years. And they were! In Daniel 9: 24-26, God prophecies through Daniel that the Messiah will come and be killed in 483 years; and He was. In Mark 8: 31, Christ stated to the disciples that the chief priests would kill Him and He would come back to life IN 3 DAYS; and He did. So why question the 1000 year Millennium?

If you give me 10 experts on the end of the earthly age, I'll give you 10 opinions. I'm not just speaking of those without prominence (like me), but seminary doctoral graduates with great intellects. I'll give you some other Bible chapters to read and help fill your data bank. Revelation 20 is the launch pad. We rule with Christ for 1000 years, having lost our sinful natures and gained our total human brilliance back. Zachariah 14 speaks of Christ's return and rule from

Jerusalem where each country is mandated to visit Him each year (or it won't rain in their country) for the balance of the 1000 years.

Isaiah 65 and 66 render the lifestyle during this period, and it's beautiful: Long life, good health, and peace amongst humans and "all" animals. Ezekiel 36-48 outlines how the future Israel will appear. Most readers have missed the giant earthquake noted in Ezekiel 38. I call the flattened area of Israel "The Jesus Pad". Zachariah 14 lists a distance of +/- 7 miles from Jerusalem to Geba; plenty of space for the new 3rd temple that the antichrist will appropriate, and I believe in the later post-Tribulation period, our Savior.

At the end of this beautiful 1000 year literal period, Satan will be released and unleashed for one last deception. People are still people with free wills. They will rebel one last time for condemnation. I'm not happy, just happy that I was saved and missed the deception. My version says that Satan is then thrown into the Lake of Fire, where the Beast and False Prophet; ARE ALSO. Friends, they were thrown there 1000 years earlier.

It then ends: "IT'S TIME"! To get to Heaven, your name must be written in the Book of Life. If so written, you depend on what Christ did. If you're in the "books", you will depend on what YOU did, and that doesn't cut it for a ticket punch to Heaven. I don't want to be thrown into the "Lake of Fire."

"IT'S TIME", my readers! God has approached you personally now. Don't reject His offer. This Bible Book is loaded with accurate promises, great and awful! Take the great one. It's still available:

RECEIVE IT, TODAY: JOHN 1:12 ☺

REVELATION REVEALED #16
CHAPTER 21
2023

Heaven Part 1

I intended to finish up with 1 "Brief" at this point in reviewing Revelation 21 and 22, but the subject is just too beautiful. I live in a gated community designed for retirees over the age of 55. The reality however is that the average age is closer to 75. As people age and literally disintegrate, one realizes that the average person thinks little or nothing about their future after death. Personally, I can't wait!

The final 4 chapters of Revelation cover the prospects for life after death in great detail. If one rejects God, our Creator, God eventually rejects you. In life, people reject neighbors, bosses, friends, and their parents. Family issues are frequent and normal. Instead of focusing on all that's been given us, we pass through a period of frustration or hurt, and focus on the negative and the attendant unhappiness. Worst of all, we tend to bring our Creator into it. God recognizes that, and has His limits. The purpose of the 2 final chapters is to point out and GLORIFY what the future holds for those who count and emphasize the blessings in life.

Chapters 19 and 20 already pointed out the future for the unappreciative!

Chapter 21 begins with: "And I saw a new heaven and a new earth; for the 1st heaven and the 1st earth had passed away…" Peter already covered earth's destruction in 2nd Peter 3: 10. If you recall Genesis 1:1, it's no big thing for God to create. Having lived in material existence during our lifetime, it's difficult/impossible for us to conceive of annihilation and re-creation! And yet, all will be new! The participants for the heavenly kingdom are mentioned in verse 7, and the uninvited are listed in verse 8.

Whatever God has in mind for this new universe, it doesn't appear to include the present one. And yet, the capital remains Jerusalem. This new creation area for heaven is 14 to 1500 miles cubed. That's huge, my friend. That's NYC to St Louis squared, and also vertical. It will have a dozen foundation stones named for the disciples and there won't be any night. The sun and moon will be gone, of course, but it's worth mentioning.

This place is so exciting that I can't wait to arrive. Paul was sure excited as he stated that "To die is gain" (Philippians 1: 21). The qualification or passport, if you will, is noted in verse 27. The jeweled beauty of this magnificent location is noted in verses 19-21. I might add the Temple is no longer around as the Trinitarian God is now the edifice. (vs 22) What an exciting destination for us repentant believers.

Since you are reading this amazing descriptive "Brief", let's just confirm your reservation in a timely fashion. Sign your name now to the:

LAMB'S BOOK OF LIFE ☺

REVELATION REVEALED #17
CHAPTER 22
2023

HEAVEN PART 2

It is said that all good things must come to an end! With God Almighty, the end is the beginning. For me, the hope of heaven is the charter map for salvation, the blueprint of ETERNITY. This finishing chapter, not only for Revelation but for the entire Bible, describes our future eternity and the reward for FAITH in the object and personage of Jesus Christ.

We see a reality we can relate to in trees that constantly bloom by rivers that flow continually. (vs 2) And we see the face of God as He rules with the Lamb from their throne. (vs 2, 3) We learn in vs 7, just who is there; repentant BELIEVERS in the God of Creation. And John is reminded to take heed as the time is near! (IT'S TIME) Jesus is coming quickly to judge each of us in a very personal way. Obviously, time is a creation of God's that He seems unaffected by, even though He has utilized it for our creation period. He, nonetheless, states His significance to that Creation in vs 13.

He then closes the entire Book of Revelation, and the entire Bible with a warning to not remove any of the dictated Words of God, including prophecies, with the admonition of separation. Separation from our Creator, is separation from eternal life with the Tree of Life. Chapters 19 and 20 indicate that all existence is eternal, even if that stage is condemnation.

So let me also state, in GLORIOUS terms, the JOY of our future in faith. The "good news" of salvation and faith in God, our Creator, is the promise of eternal existence in this unbelievable (if you will) domain, with our Creator God. I might add that we will be back to full intellect, and without a sinful nature. We will have no inclination to activate any infractions toward our Creator or one another. Paradise? You bet! And why? Because the Bible (Word of God) says so!

Everything in my life has been the motivation to "look ahead". It's driven my hope, my energy, and my activities. I see no reason to depart from that paradigm considering the life after. God's inclusion of the Heavenly topic fits right into that pattern. I then close this scenario of "Briefs" as God, the author closes it with:

THE HOPE OF HEAVEN! ☺

www.ingramcontent.com/pod-product-compliance
Lightning Source LLC
Chambersburg PA
CBHW032112170626
46808CB00008B/3027